The Case of the
Spooky Sleepover

Read all the Jigsaw Jones Mysteries

The Case of the
Spooky Sleepover

by James Preller
illustrated by John Speirs
cover illustration by R. W. Alley

A
LITTLE APPLE
PAPERBACK

SCHOLASTIC INC.
New York Toronto London Auckland Sydney
Mexico City New Delhi Hong Kong

For
Mike & Mary

Book design by Dawn Adelman

ISBN 0-590-69129-5

Text copyright © 1999 by James Preller. Illustrations copyright © 1999 by Scholastic Inc. All rights reserved. Published by Scholastic Inc. SCHOLASTIC, LITTLE APPLE PAPERBACKS, and associated logos are trademarks and/or registered trademarks of Scholastic Inc.

24 23 22 21 20 19 18 17 16 15 14 13   1 2 3 4/0

Printed in the U.S.A.   40
First Scholastic printing, March 1999

CONTENTS

Chapter One
Ralphie Jordan

Ralphie Jordan was the most popular kid in room 201. Everybody liked Ralphie. And Ralphie liked everybody right back. He had dark eyes, dark skin, dark hair — and he was as thin as a flagpole. Best of all, Ralphie Jordan was a world-champion smiler. Nobody had a bigger smile or used it more often.

Only today, Ralphie wasn't smiling.

He plopped down next to me in the school cafeteria. "Hey, Jigsaw," he said. "Can I talk to you for a minute?"

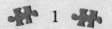 1

It's hard to talk with peanut butter in your mouth. I know. I've tried it. "Mmuffurf," I mumbled. I reached for my milk and swallowed hard. "Whew," I said. "That's better."

Ralphie flashed a toothy grin. But the smile left his face in a hurry, as if it had somewhere else to go. That wasn't a good sign. Something has to be wrong if Ralphie Jordan doesn't smile. "What's the matter?" I asked. "Bologna again?"

"Nah, nothing like that," Ralphie said. And as if to prove it, he poured out his lunch bag on the table. Then he lined up everything in a neat row. Ralphie had a ham sandwich, a plastic bag of grapes, two Oreo cookies, a carrot, and a juice box. He picked up the ham sandwich and squished it between his hands. By the time he was done, the sandwich was flatter than Flat Stanley. Ralphie took a few big bites of the sandwich, then twisted open an Oreo. He licked the white insides. "You're still a detective, right?" he asked.

"Sure," I answered. "For a dollar a day, I make problems go away."

Ralphie didn't say anything. He was busy working on his second Oreo. I waited. In the detective business, things go better when you sit back and listen. So that's what I did.

Finally Ralphie spoke up. "Can you keep a secret?" he whispered.

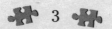 3

"I can," I said. "But when I'm on a case, I share the facts with Mila Yeh. We're partners, you know."

Ralphie thought that over. He shrugged. "I don't know. It's sort of goofy."

I waited for the goofy part to come.

It came.

"Jigsaw," Ralphie asked, "do you believe in ghosts?"

Chapter Two
On Top of Spaghetti

"Ghosts?" I repeated. "Like Casper the Friendly?"

Ralphie Jordan shook his head. "No, the *unfriendly* kind."

Maybe it was the look on his face. Maybe a window was open and a cold breeze blew down my back. But I got a creepy feeling. Like watching a scary movie with the lights out.

"Ghosts aren't real," I told him. The truth was, I didn't know for sure. But one thing was certain. I didn't want Ralphie Jordan to

 5

think I was scared. No one needs a fraidy-cat detective.

Ralphie sort of frowned. Then he gave me a big, easy smile. A Ralphie Jordan Special. But I knew it was just an act.

"What's this about?" I asked. "You haven't seen a ghost, have you?"

"Forget it," Ralphie said. "It's probably nothing."

"Sure, probably nothing," I agreed. "But if you want to talk, I'll be in my tree house after school. Come by if you feel like it."

"Thanks, Jigsaw," Ralphie said. "I think I will." Then Ralphie pointed to his uneaten lunch — the carrot, grapes, and juice. "Want it?" he asked.

I didn't and I told him so. Ralphie stuffed his leftovers into his lunch bag. He crumpled the bag into a tight ball. Then he stood up, turned, and fired. The bag floated toward the garbage can.

Swish.

"Yes!" Ralphie called out in a fake announcer's voice. "Jordan shoots . . . and scores!"

After Ralphie left, I pulled out my detective journal. I ripped out a piece of paper and wrote a message to Mila. We wrote all our messages in code. I decided to use a space code. All I had to do was write out the message without putting spaces between the words. It looked like this:

MEETMEATTHETREEHOUSEAFTERSCHOOL.

I looked it over. Too easy, I decided. So I took out another piece of paper and tried again. I added spaces in the wrong places. Now it looked pretty tricky.

ME ETMEA TTHETRE EHOU SEAFTERSC HOOL.

Mila needed to find the real words and draw lines to separate them. When Mila was done, it should look like this:

ME ET/ ME/ A T/ THE/ TRE E/ HOU SE/ AFTER/ SC HOOL.

I found Mila sitting with Lucy Hiller and Bigs Maloney. Lucy was eating today's hot-lunch special. It was spaghetti and meatballs. At least, they *looked* like meatballs. They probably *tasted* more like golf balls. How Lucy ate the stuff was a mystery to me. Yeesh.

Mila was singing. That was normal. You'd have to put a sock in her mouth to keep Mila from singing. Our teacher, Ms. Gleason, taught the song to us in class. It sounded like "On Top of Old Smokey," but the words were different.

Lucy and Bigs giggled while Mila sang.

"On top of spaghetti,
All covered with cheese,
I lost my poor meatball,
When somebody sneezed."

I said hi and handed Mila the note. She stuffed the paper into her pocket without looking at it. Then the bell rang.

Lunch was over.

But the case was just beginning.

Chapter Three
Room 201 Goes Batty

Back in room 201, Ms. Gleason told us, "This afternoon we're going to study a nocturnal animal." She looked around the classroom. "Would anyone like to tell us what *nocturnal* means?"

Bobby Solofsky yelled out, "It's an animal that sleeps all day and stays out all night!"

Ms. Gleason ignored him. She didn't like it when we called out answers — even when it was the right answer. She called on Danika Starling instead. "Thank you for raising your hand, Danika." As usual, Danika knew the right answer.

"Yesterday we talked about owls," Ms. Gleason said. "Today we're going to learn about bats."

"Yeah, I love baseball!" Ralphie Jordan joked.

Even Ms. Gleason had to laugh. Besides, it was hard to get mad at Ralphie Jordan — even when he didn't raise his hand. We talked about what we already knew about bats. Then we gathered in the reading circle. Ms. Gleason read a book called *Bats! Bats! and More Bats!* It had really cool pictures.

We broke into groups and made Venn diagrams, comparing bats to owls. They were a lot alike. Most bats and owls were predators. They hunted at night. We also listed the ways they were different. That was pretty easy, too. Owls are birds. They have feathers. Bats are mammals. They just *think* they're birds.

Later on, we made little brown bat stick puppets. It was fun. Except I sort of made a mess with the glue. I spilled some on the floor. Helen Zuckerman stepped in it. She was sort of upset.

Oh, well. Nobody's perfect.

Before cleanup, Ms. Gleason reminded us about the field trip on Monday. We were going to Four Rivers Nature Preserve. We were going to take a bus, and two parents were coming with us.

Everybody had to be prepared for rainy weather. Ms. Gleason said that we were going *rain or shine*. "Spring is right around the corner," Ms. Gleason said. "That means a lot of rain, because all those flowers and trees need water to grow."

Bigs Maloney said he hoped it would rain. That's Bigs for you. He's a stomping-in-puddles kind of guy.

"What will we do when we get there?" Joey Pignattano asked.

Everybody knew the answer. Even Joey. But it was like a good story. We wanted to hear it again.

"A guide will lead us on a hike around a beaver pond," Ms. Gleason reminded us. "We'll look at animal habitats. Where they live, what they eat. We'll *observe* and *draw conclusions*."

"How do you draw a conclusion?" I piped up. "With crayons?" Everybody laughed.

Except for Ms. Gleason. "Excuse me, Theodore Jones," she said. "I'm very tired of people talking while I'm talking." Ms. Gleason rubbed her eyes and her body sort of sagged. I guess she really was tired. Ms. Gleason took a deep breath. "We'll have a wonderful day. We'll have a picnic. And if the weather cooperates, we'll end the trip with a treasure hunt."

We couldn't wait. Sure, it wasn't Hoffberg's Playland, but a walk in the woods sure beat school.

"Okay, boys and girls," Ms. Gleason said. "It's been a long, hard week. Time for our Friday Cheer. Are you ready to scream your heads off?"

We sure were.

Ms. Gleason counted down, "Five . . . four . . . three . . . two . . . one!"

For ten seconds, we screamed our heads off. We hooted. We howled. We hollered and shouted. We shrieked. We screeched. We stomped, whomped, and roared. We yelled. We bellowed. And finally, we mellowed.

What a way to end the week!

Chapter Four

In the Tree House

When the weather was good, I used the tree house in my backyard as an office. Sure, maybe it wasn't the greatest place ever built. It was lopsided and it wobbled just enough to make you nervous. But it didn't matter to me. What mattered was . . . *it was mine*. See, the tree house was supposed to be for all the kids in my family — Billy, Hillary, Nicholas, Daniel, and me. But I've pretty much taken it over.

I climbed up and waited for Mila and Ralphie. I set out a pitcher of grape juice

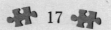

and three cups. I took a sip. Suddenly Mila's head popped up. "BOO!" she shouted.

Grape juice squirted out my nose. "Mila! You could have given me a heart attack. Yeesh!"

"Lighten up, Jigsaw," Mila said. "I was just practicing my sneak attacks. Pretty good, huh?"

I admitted that she was a good sneak. "But next time," I said, "practice on someone else."

Mila grinned.

"Hey," I asked, "why didn't Rags bark?"

"I gave him half a pretzel," Mila said. "That kept him quiet."

That was Rags for you. If you fed him once, he'd love you forever. I didn't mind. It was nice that Mila and Rags were becoming friends. See, Mila is allergic to fur. She had to stay far away from Rags. But Mila started taking a new allergy medicine. It worked. I was glad. All that sneezing can get on a guy's nerves.

I told Mila about my talk with Ralphie Jordan. She listened closely. Just then, Ralphie peddled into my backyard. He leaned his bicycle against the tree. Rags watched from his doghouse and barked twice. For Rags, that was his idea of making a big fuss.

Ralphie climbed the ladder. He fished a torn, crumpled dollar from his pocket. "Hold on to your money," I told him.

"I don't even know what you want me to do."

"I want you to make my problem go away," he said.

"What sort of problem?" Mila asked.

Ralphie glanced at Mila, then back at me. "She won't laugh?"

"Not unless you tickle her feet with a feather," I answered. I pulled out my detective journal. I wrote:

Friday, March 20th.
Client: Ralphie Jordan.

"Go ahead," Mila urged. "Nobody will laugh at you."

Ralphie took a long, slow sip of grape juice. "My house is haunted," he said.

Chapter Five

The Scream of the Crime

I poured myself another drink.

Ralphie continued, "When I go to bed, I hear weird noises."

"It's probably just the wind," Mila explained.

"Does the wind go *scritch-scratch* against the walls?" Ralphie asked. "Does the wind go *thump, thump, thump*? Does it rattle chains and moan in the middle of the night?"

"Maybe it's just a nighttime animal," I offered.

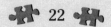

"Yes," Mila said. "It could be a nocturnal animal. Like an owl or a raccoon or . . ."

". . . or a moose!" I added.

"What?!" Mila asked.

I wiggled my fingers behind my head, like antlers. "You know," I explained. "A moose."

Mila shook her head and sighed. She faced Ralphie. "What did the moan sound like?"

Ralphie cupped his hands in front of his mouth. He started to moan — a long, low, spooky moan. "*WooOOoowoo. WOOoowooOOoo.*"

That was good enough for me. I opened my journal. I grabbed a marker and drew a picture of the suspect. It didn't exactly look like a ghost. Instead, I'd say it was a pretty good drawing of an upside-down sock . . . with eyes. Yeesh.

I looked at Ralphie, then nodded toward my glass jar. Ralphie poked the dollar into the jar.

"What now?" Ralphie asked.

"Now," Mila said, "we visit the scene of the crime."

We made it to Ralphie's in three minutes. His house, like spring, was just around the corner.

Ralphie lived in the biggest, oldest house on the block. It was two stories, with a high, sloping roof. Ralphie brought us onto the front porch. *Creak, creeeeak.* The chains of a bench swing groaned in the wind. "My mother's visiting cousins in Georgia," Ralphie said. "My father works at home. But I'm not allowed to bother him unless it's a real emergency."

He brought us upstairs into his bedroom. It was a large room with dark paneling on the walls. On one side the ceiling came

down in a sharp angle. It made the room feel cozy, like a cave.

"I see you like scary stories," Mila said, eyeing the bookshelves. She tilted her head and read some titles out loud. "*In a Dark, Dark Room. The Haunting of Grade Three. The Ghost in the Attic.*"

I looked out the window into Ralphie's backyard. There was a garden below. And beyond that, a lone willow tree on a green lawn. Off to the right, his brother, Justin,

was shooting hoops in the driveway. "Hey, Mila," I said. "I can see your house from here."

Mila came to the window. "You're right, Jigsaw. See that window? That's my room."

I turned away and prowled Ralphie's bedroom with my eyes. Everything seemed normal. "Well," I said. "I don't see any signs of a ghost."

"What did you expect?" Ralphie said. "Ghosts are nocturnal. They only walk the earth at night."

"Well, there's nothing else to do," Mila concluded. She folded her arms. "Jigsaw has to spend the night."

"I do?" I said. "But . . ."

"Great — a sleepover!" Ralphie yelled. "I'll go ask my dad."

Oh, brother. I always get the dirty work.

Chapter Six
The Sleepover

Saturday afternoon, I picked up the phone and dialed.

"Hello?" a voice answered.

"Is Ralphie there?"

"Excuse me?" the voice asked. It was Mr. Jordan.

I tried again. "Is Ralphie home . . . *please*?" All I heard was silence. Then I added, "This is Jigsaw."

"That's much better, Jigsaw," Mr. Jordan said. "Hold on. I'll get him for you."

I told Ralphie it might be a good idea if Rags slept over, too. "He usually sleeps in my room," I said. "He'd be scared without me."

Ralphie was thrilled. He asked his father. Mr. Jordan said it was fine with him. I knew it would be. Ralphie's dad was a dog person. When we were on vacation in Florida, the Jordans watched Rags for a whole week. And they didn't even hate it.

I took a bath and even used soap. My hair was washed and combed. My socks were matched. My underwear was clean. I was everything a detective should be. Until I tried on my new secondhand pants.

"Mom!" I yelled down the stairs. "I am NOT wearing Nick's old jeans."

My mom climbed the stairs, muttering. "What are you talking about?" she said. "You look fine." She rolled up the pant legs. "There, that's better!"

"Mom, they're too baggy. I can't go to Ralphie's like this. I look like Shaggy on *Scooby-Doo*."

"Those jeans are perfectly fine."

"But . . ."

"No buts, Theodore," she said.

"But . . ."

Then she gave me . . . the look.

It meant: *End of discussion.*

Oh, brother.

I threw my things into a backpack. Toothbrush, pajamas, detective journal,

extra markers, a water bowl and a bone for Rags. Then I went downstairs and grabbed the house flashlight. I didn't ask permission. It was too big a risk. My mom might have said no.

Ralphie and his brother, Justin, were playing catch on his front lawn. Justin Jordan was fifteen years old. He was tall and strong and he could run like the wind. He loved sports. Any sport. Sometimes Justin teased us, but he was usually pretty nice . . . for a teenager.

Justin bent down and gave Rags a playful push. "Hey, Ragsy. Remember me?" he asked. Rags answered by wagging his tail. He remembered.

"Rags is sleeping over, too," Ralphie told Justin. "He's going to be our watchdog."

"Watchdog?" said Justin. "What for?"

Ralphie looked around. He whispered, "You know. What I told you about. *The ghost.*"

Justin laughed out loud. "Ghost!" he said. "Don't be ridiculous. Ghosts aren't real. It's just your imagination."

Ralphie wasn't buying a word of it. "Go ahead, don't believe me," he said. "See if I care. But you'll be sorry when he sneaks into *your* room and scares *you* to death."

Chapter Seven
The Ghost Story

Mila joined us at Ralphie's house for pizza dinner. Later we played Frisbee football in the backyard. The teams were Justin and Mila against me and Ralphie. I'd like to say we won. But I can't. Because we lost.

Mostly, though, we waited for the ghost to come. We watched as the sun fell from the sky. Long shadows filled the backyard. The wind started to blow. Leaves danced in the trees. And like a woolly blanket, darkness wrapped around us.

Mr. Jordan came out onto the porch. "Okay, kids," he said. "It's getting late and it looks like a storm is kicking up. Better come inside."

Before Mila left, we went over the plan one more time. We were going to use flashlights to signal each other from the windows. Three short flashes meant we were okay. Two long flashes meant . . . trouble.

"What do I do if it's two long flashes?" Mila asked.

"Call the ghostbusters," Ralphie joked.

Nobody laughed. "You'll think of something," I told her.

Suddenly the sky burst with rain. It poured. It rained cats. It rained dogs. It rained hippos and elephants, too. The rain got so bad, Mr. Jordan had to give Mila a ride home — even though she only lived around the corner.

Mr. Jordan let us stay up to watch a

video called *Zombies Ate New Jersey*. He even made popcorn for us. There wasn't much else to do after that but go into Ralphie's room and wait for the ghost. We laid our sleeping bags on the floor. Rags curled up in the corner of the room.

"I'm not very sleepy," I said. "Are you?"

Ralphie sat up with a smile. "No way, José!"

There was a knock on the door. "You guys still awake?" It was Justin. He came

into the room carrying a box. "Any sign of that ghost?" he asked.

"Not yet," Ralphie said.

Justin sat cross-legged on the floor. He placed the box in front of him. "Well, I hate to spoil your little sleepover, but there's no such thing as a ghost." Justin paused. Then he leaned forward and said, "But if you want, I *could* tell you a spooky story."

I looked at Ralphie. He nodded. Yes.

Justin looked around the room and

frowned. "Not dark enough," he said. He turned off one light, then another. I could barely see his face.

"Wait a minute," Ralphie said. He turned on my flashlight and pointed it away from us. Eerie shapes perched on the wall, like a row of black crows.

"Once upon a time . . ." Justin began. He spoke softly, in a whisper. We leaned forward to hear. ". . . on this very spot. Long, long ago. A man was killed."

I felt Ralphie grab my wrist.

"I know this is true," Justin said. "Because I found this box when I was digging near the old willow tree." He put his hand on the box. "But I'm sure you don't want me to open it. Do you?"

Ralphie nodded again. Yes. He did.

Nobody asked me.

Justin reached over and turned off the flashlight.

Suddenly it was as dark as a mummy's tomb.

Justin opened the box. . . .

Chapter Eight

Eyeballs in the Dark

It was too dark to see. I listened closely and felt Ralphie's body pressed close to mine.

"In this box," Justin said, "is the rotting flesh of the man's dead body."

"For real?" I asked.

"*Shhhh*," Ralphie hushed.

Nah, I thought. It can't be for real. It's just a story.

"Put out your hands," Justin said. He placed two round, slippery balls into my fingers. They felt like marbles, but squishier.

"Those were his eyes."

Yeesh. I handed the eyeballs to Ralphie.

Justin gave me something else. It was small and soft and a little bumpy. It bent in my fingers.

"That was his ear."

My stomach felt funny. I handed the ear to Ralphie.

"This is the worst, most disgusting, most

horrible part," Justin whispered. "You're not scared, are you?"

We didn't answer. I don't even know if we breathed.

"Here. I've put it on the floor," Justin whispered. "Feel for it." Ralphie's hands and mine fumbled in the dark. I felt something slimy. In the darkness, I tried to figure out the shape. It had long, curved pieces, like fat worms. I counted them.

One, two, three, four . . .

Justin said, "It was . . ."

". . . his HAND!" I shouted.

"Aaaaaaarrrggghhh!" Ralphie screamed. He jumped up and flicked on the lights.

Justin fell back on the floor, laughing.

With the lights on, we could see the body parts.

The "eyes" were two peeled grapes.

The "ear" was a dried apricot.

The "hand" was a rubber glove filled with mud.

Still laughing, Justin picked himself up off the floor and strolled to the door. "Chill out, guys. That's the only scare you're gonna get tonight. There's no such thing as a ghost."

I was glad to see Justin leave.

Maybe now I'd stop trembling.

Suddenly I remembered. "Mila!" We rushed to the window. It was still raining, but not as hard as before. We signaled three times. Nothing happened. We did it again. We searched through the darkness. Nothing.

"Look!" Ralphie finally cried. There it was, three flashes in the window. It was Mila.

Once again, we got into our sleeping bags and turned off the lights. "Hey, Jigsaw," Ralphie said. "Want to hear a joke?"

"Sure."

"What do ghosts eat for dessert?" he asked.

"I dunno," I answered.

"Ice scream!" Even in the dark, I could make out Ralphie's bright white smile. Then he yawned.

A minute passed. "You sleepy, Ralphie?" I asked. "Ralphie?"

He was out like a light.

Oh, brother. I lay awake in a dark, dark room, thinking that this was one of Mila's worst ideas ever. And I tried to fall asleep. I mean, I *really* tried. But all I could think of was ghosts . . . and eyeballs . . . and creepy noises.

Scritch-scratch.

Nah, just the wind, I told myself.

Scritch. Scritch. Scraaaatch.

The noise seemed to come from the wall nearest me. I tried to forget about it by humming a happy tune. *Hum-de-dum, de-dum-dum.*

Then it started. Just as Ralphie had described it.

WooOOoowooOOoowooOOoo.

I lifted my head and looked around the room. Soon there were more sounds. *Thump. Thump. Thump.* I looked up. In the corner of the room, I saw two yellow eyes.

They were floating in the dark.

Scritch-scratch. Thump, thump, thump. WooOO-wooOOoo.

The eyes were coming closer.

And closer.

Right then, I knew for sure:

I was a goner.

Chapter Nine

The Night Visitor

SLURP!

A giant tongue licked my face.

"Ragsy, old pal!" I said. The floating eyes were his! My big, friendly, drooling, ever-loving dog! I was never so happy to get licked in all my life.

My happiness quickly vanished when I heard a scream. It came from downstairs. Then nothing. Just dead silence.

Don't ask me why. But I *had* to see what it was. I grabbed my flashlight. Ralphie was still sleeping. "Come on, Rags," I whispered.

My big, brave dog clip-clopped across the floor. At that moment, I was glad Rags wasn't a French poodle. I crept down the darkened stairway. *Thump, thump, thump.* I stopped to listen. Whew. It was only the pounding of my heart. Then I heard another shout. A muffled voice cried, "Get him! Get him!"

I jumped when a hand suddenly grabbed my shoulder. . . .

"Jigsaw, what's up?"

I turned. It was Ralphie.

I put a finger to my lips. "I think it's somewhere down there."

"What's down there?" Ralphie asked. He was still half asleep.

"The ghost," I whispered.

"NO! NO!" begged the voice.

Ralphie smiled. "Oh, that's just my

father," he said. "He's probably watching a basketball game. He always shouts at the players."

Just then, Rags bolted down the stairs, through the living room, and into the den. Mr. Jordan, holding a bowl of pretzels, came out to the bottom of the stairs. He squinted into the flashlight. "Ralph? Jigsaw? Turn that flashlight off, will you? What are you doing up at this hour?" Rags stood by his side, hoping for a pretzel.

Ralphie stammered, "Um . . ."

"Rags needs water," I said.

Mr. Jordan gave us a funny look. He gave Rags a pretzel. "Okay, boys. Then right back into bed. No more funny stuff."

We went into the kitchen. I gave Rags some water. He lapped it up. Then I searched the cupboards. I found what I needed above the sink. It was a box of Rice Krispies. "Can we take this upstairs?" I asked Ralphie.

"I guess so," he said. "Why?"

"You'll see," I answered.

Back in Ralphie's room, I gave Rags a bone to keep him busy. Then I poured the cereal on the floor. "This is a ghost alarm," I said. "If the ghost comes into the room when we're sleeping . . ."

". . . we'll hear *snap, crackle, pop!*" Ralphie said.

For the third time that night, we crawled back into our sleeping bags. We kept all the lights on. I must have fallen asleep, because I woke to a noise. It was a step.

Then another. Then another. Louder and louder. Closer and closer.

I woke Ralphie. "Something's coming," I whispered.

The doorknob slowly, slowly turned. *Eeeek*. The door opened.

After that, a lot of stuff happened at once. Things got pretty mixed-up. Ralphie pulled the sleeping bag over his head and started screaming, "Don't eat me! Don't eat me! Don't eat me!"

Rags started running around the room in circles, barking like crazy.

I looked up and saw Mr. Jordan at the door. He looked pretty scared himself. He came into the room — *crunch, crunch, snap, crackle, pop, crunch* — and started waving his arms around.

I hollered at the top of my lungs, "RAGS, BE QUIET!"

After a while, Ralphie stopped screaming.

Rags stopped barking.

And Mr. Jordan just stood there with his hands on his hips. He looked at Ralphie. He looked at me. He looked at Rags. He looked at the Rice Krispies on the floor. Then his head swung back to Ralphie, then back to me. Mr. Jordan didn't move for a long, long time. He sighed. He ran his strong fingers over his mustache. He sighed again.

"Is everyone calm?" he finally asked.

We nodded. Rags wagged.

"Ralph, Jigsaw," Mr. Jordan slowly said. "I want you to come with me. And boys," he added, before leading us down the hall, "you had best clean up this mess in the morning."

Finally, at long last, we fell asleep. All of us. Me, Ralphie, and Rags. Huddled together. Snug as bugs in a rug.

In Mr. Jordan's very crowded — and very safe — king-size bed.

Chapter Ten

Nature Detectives

I woke up early on Sunday. Mr. Jordan made waffles while Ralphie and I cleaned Ralphie's room. Sweeping up all those Rice Krispies made us hungry. After breakfast, I went home. I needed a nap.

On Monday, we headed to Four Rivers Nature Preserve for our field trip. It felt good to get away from ghosts for a while.

Mila sat on the bus next to me. "I think I saw something the other night," she told me. "In Ralphie's backyard."

"What do you mean . . . *saw something*?" I asked.

Mila leaned close to me. "I kept trying to signal you with my flashlight. But you didn't answer, except for that one time." She paused. "I saw a shape moving around."

"What kind of shape?" I asked.

Mila shook her head. "I couldn't tell. It was too dark. But it might have been a person."

"Or a ghost," I added.

The bus came to a stop.

I was surprised when I saw our guide. I expected somebody with a big ranger hat. But this guy had a magnifying glass and a hat like Sherlock Holmes! His name was Hal Roberts. He brought us into the Nature Center. It was a small museum. In the back room, there was a large window overlooking a field. We all took turns with the binoculars, looking at the birds in the feeders. The best part, though, was Aristotle. He was in a glass cage set into the wall. Mr. Roberts told us that Aristotle was a white-barred owl.

He told us a sad story. A couple of years ago, a nice lady found Aristotle on the side of the road. The owl had been hit by a car and was badly injured. She took Aristotle to an animal doctor. The doctor saved Aristotle's life. But Aristotle lost a wing in the accident. He would never fly again.

Now he lived at Four Rivers, stuck inside a cage for the rest of his life. I felt bad for Aristotle. Ralphie and I tried to cheer him up with a few hoots.

Aristotle didn't give a hoot back. I guess I didn't blame him.

Then we started our hike. It was called the Beaver Pond Trail. After a little while, Mr. Roberts made us stop and look at something. It was a pile of brown pellets. In other words, deer poop!

Mr. Roberts told us we were lucky. "With all that rain this weekend, the ground is nice and muddy. Perfect for animal tracks." He asked us to become nature detectives. We had to look around for signs of animal life. He called them clues.

"I think I found something!" Mila shouted.

"Good detective work," Mr. Roberts said. "This is an animal track." Mr. Roberts pointed out the hoofprints. He said it was a deer track. He poured plaster of paris into the track. "When the plaster hardens, it will form a mold. Then you can take it back to your classroom."

"For keeps?" Geetha asked.

"For keeps," Mr. Roberts answered.

It was a great day. Mr. Roberts taught us to look closely at things. He pointed to a row of holes on a tree. We had to guess what kind of animal made the holes. Helen Zuckerman guessed that it was a woodpecker. She was right.

After the hike, we had a big picnic. Ms. Gleason let us run around and act wild. Then we had a scavenger hunt. We had to use our skills as nature detectives to find all sorts of things. I found something that told us the wind was blowing. That was easy — the leaves on the trees. Mila found empty acorns. We drew the conclusion that they had been eaten by something. Probably a squirrel. Ralphie even discovered a

bird's nest. But we weren't allowed to touch it.

In the end, we learned that nature tells us stories. But nature doesn't use words. Nature tells us in its own language.

It really was like being a detective. If you looked at things closely enough, the clues would tell you a story.

Chapter Eleven
The Mysterious Footprints

We decided to play nature detective as soon as we got home from the field trip. Ralphie's yard was the biggest, so that's where we went. But first I stopped home to get my magnifying glass. We looked for animal clues. I guess Ralphie found the first clue. He stepped in dog poop.

I patted Ralphie on the back. "Nice work, Detective."

While Ralphie changed into sneakers, Mila and I searched the garden for animal tracks. Mila found a centipede. I let it crawl on my hand. Only it didn't crawl much. After a while, we decided it was probably dead. Yeesh.

"Hey, Jigsaw," Mila said. "Look at this." She was behind the bushes, next to the house. Mila picked up a broom. "What's this doing here?" she asked.

I held up my magnifying glass. The broom was caked with clumps of dry mud. Looking down, I suddenly shouted, "Footprints!" Ralphie joined us as we gathered around the mysterious footprints.

"Any conclusions?" I asked.

Ralphie shrugged. "I guess somebody walked back here."

"But why?" I said. "There's nothing here." We thought it over for a while.

"What about that strange shape you saw the other night?" I asked Mila.

"Yes," she said. "It was right around this area."

Suddenly I understood everything. The broom . . . Mila's mysterious shape . . . the large footprint. The clues were coming together.

And they were telling a ghost story.

I gazed up at the side of the house. Up high, near Ralphie's window, I saw tiny streaks of mud. "Let me try something," I said. I held the broom high and rubbed it against the wall. We listened closely.

Scritch. Scratch.

I banged the broom against the wall.

Thump. Thump. Thump.

"I understand now," Ralphie said. "The ghost used this broom to make the scary sounds."

Mila knelt beside the footprints and stared through the magnifying glass. "I don't think so," she said. "Unless you know any ghosts who wear Nikes."

We sent Ralphie inside. He came back in a minute . . . holding a pair of Justin's sneakers. "It was easy," Ralphie explained. "Justin left them in the mudroom."

As I suspected, the sneakers were Nikes. And they were muddy and damp. I turned a sneaker upside down and held it next to the footprint. "A perfect match," I said.

I put my hand on Ralphie's shoulder. "You don't have a ghost," I told him. "You have something far worse." I paused. "You have a *teenager.*"

Ralphie asked, "But how did Justin make the *woo-woo* noises?"

"I'm not positive," I answered. "Probably the same way you did, back at the tree house." I cupped my hands over my mouth. "*WooOOoowooOOoowooOOoo.*"

The three of us marched into Ralphie's house. Justin was eating a bowl of cereal in the kitchen. I held the broom in my hands. Mila held the sneakers. And Ralphie pointed at his brother. "You're the ghost!"

Chapter Twelve
Justin Gets All Wet

Justin confessed everything.

"But why?" Ralphie asked. "You scared me to death."

Justin smiled. "Admit it," he said. "You loved it."

And I guess Justin was right. It was fun thinking there was a ghost on the loose. Sort of.

Of course, we still had to get him back. Fair is fair. And I knew just how to do it, too. It was an old prank my father showed me. About half an hour later, we found

Justin in his bedroom. He was lying on the floor with his head between the stereo speakers.

"Want us to show you a trick?" Ralphie asked.

Justin said, "Nah, too busy."

"Come on," Ralphie urged. "You owe me."

Justin groaned and stood up. I stepped forward, holding a small bucket of water. I said, "I can make this bucket stick like magic to the ceiling. Want to see?"

I climbed up on Justin's desk. I mumbled some fancy mumbo jumbo. Stretching on my toes, I held the bucket of water against the ceiling. "It takes a minute to stick," I explained. After a little while, I told Justin that my arm was getting tired. "You're the strongest," I said. "Could you please hold this for a while?"

Justin groaned. "Better yet," I said. "Just grab that hockey stick. You can stand underneath it and hold it from there."

Justin grabbed the stick. I did my best not to smile. He pressed it firmly against the bucket. I climbed down. Mila and Ralphie giggled. Then we said, "Thanks a lot, Justin. See you later!"

We ran out the door, leaving Justin in the room standing under a bucket of water. "Hey, guys! When are you coming back?" he yelled. "Hey, get back here! What do I do with the bucket?!"

We ran into the backyard, laughing our

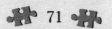 71

heads off. In a few minutes, Justin came out to find us. His shirt looked wet. But he was smiling. "Nice trick, you guys," he said. "I suppose I deserved it."

Just then, Mr. Jordan pulled into the driveway. Justin looked at his father. He looked back at us.

There was a twinkle in his eye.

Justin walked toward the car. "Hey, Dad," Justin called out. "Want to see how I can make a bucket of water stick to the ceiling?"

Ralphie turned to me and smiled. It was a Ralphie Jordan Special.

Well, that's it, I thought. For a dollar a day, I make ghosts go away. Another mystery solved. It was like a puzzle with all the pieces in place. Nothing to do now but rip it up and start on another one. I knew there would be more cases. More mysteries to solve. And I'd be waiting — ready to piece the clues together.

That's why they call me Jigsaw.